123
SESAME STREET

Brought to You by... Sesame Street!

#1

By Kara McMahon
Illustrated by Joe Mathieu, Richard Walz,
Mary Beth Nelson, and Susan Greenstein

Random House 🏠 New York

Published in the United States by Random House Children's Books, a division of Random House, Inc., New York, NY 10019,
and simultaneously in Canada by Random House of Canada Limited, Toronto, in conjunction with Sesame Workshop.
Sesame Street, Sesame Workshop, and their logos are trademarks and service marks of Sesame Workshop.
www.randomhouse.com/kids/sesame   www.sesameworkshop.org
ISBN 0-375-82844-3 (trade) — ISBN 0-375-92844-8 (lib. bdg.)
Library of Congress Control Number: 2003107406
MANUFACTURED IN MEXICO   10 9 8 7 6 5 4 3
RANDOM HOUSE and colophon are registered trademarks of Random House, Inc.

Journey to Ernie,
starring Ernie and Big Bird

Illustrated by Richard Walz and Joe Mathieu

Letter of the Day,
Starring Cookie Monster

Illustrated by Richard Walz

The Sesame Street Story of the Day,
starring Elmo and Zoe

Illustrated by Richard Walz
Written by Abigail Tabby

Global Grover

Illustrated by Susan Greenstein

Spanish Word of the Day,
starring Rosita

Illustrated by Richard Walz

Number of the Day,
starring the Count

Illustrated by Joe Mathieu

Elmo's World

Illustrated by Mary Beth Nelson

Hello, everybodee! This is your furry pal **Grover,** here to give you a tour of *Sesame Street.*

I, Grover, am a monster with a lifetime of experience living on Sesame Street, so I am highly qualified for the job. Oh, you are so lucky!

Before we begin, I will teach you how to read a book. You simply turn the page with your cute and adorable fingers. . . . But wait. I do not want you to turn the page yet. Just pretend. Very good! You are an excellent pretend page-turner.

Now it is time to turn the page. Turn *now.*

Psst! Over here! I, Grover, am hiding from Big Bird. Big Bird will never find me here! Oh, I am so smart!

B. BIRD

10, 9, 8, 7, 6, 5, 4,

Oh, hello out there! And hello to you, Grover. Thanks for coming by. It's time to play "Journey to Ernie"! I can't wait for us to find out where Ernie is hiding today.

When you turn the page, he will be hiding somewhere in the picture and we'll have to find him. Ernie is a pretty tricky fellow, so we might not find him right away. And that's okay!

Will you count with me?

And now that you have counted, it is time to turn the page.

3, 2, 1!

I see a tiger that looks a lot like Ernie.
Do you see it?

That's not Ernie, though.
Let's keep looking.

Look at that parrot.
I thought he was
Ernie, too!

hat coconut looks
ally familiar!

Coming up next . . .
the Letter of the Day!

und Ernie! Can you find him?

I, Grover, have made sure that Cookie Monster cannot eat the Letter of the Day cookie by hiding it safely inside a paper bag. I hid the paper bag in the pile of cookies, where I am certain Cookie Monster will never find it.

DO NOT EAT

Me have very big dilemma! Me no want to eat Letter of the Day cookie, but me cannot remember what the Letter of the Day is. So me not know which cookie not to eat. And me SO HUNGRY!

Me will sort through alphabet, cookie by cookie, until me remember Letter of the Day. Me sure that A, B, C, D, and E are not Letter of the Day cookie, so me will eat JUST these five cookies. . . .

COOOOKIES!!!!! Me cannot stop! Have to eat every single COOOOKIE!!!

Now me remember!

Letter of the Day is letter F. Cookie was safe all along. Beautiful letter F. F for "friend." Me want to eat funny, friendly, flavorful letter F cookie right now! *Crunch, crunch!*

And I thought the Letter of the Day was safe, hidden in those cookies. Oh, I am so embarrassed! Time to turn the page.

Thank you, Cookie Monster!

Speaking of cookies, you may be wondering why I, Grover, am holding cookies and teacups and a pail and shovel. The story you are going to read about my friends Elmo and Zoe is about tea and cookies . . . and pails and shovels. That is the reason I am holding these things.

So, without further ado, we bring you the story "Elmo and Zoe Are (Still) Friends."

Zoe was excited! Elmo was coming to her house and they were going to play tea party. She had everything set up.

"Ready to go to the playground?" Elmo asked when he got there.

"The playground? No way, Elmo!" Zoe said. "I'm all set for our tea party! See?"

"But Elmo has everything for the sandbox!" said Elmo, holding up his sand toys. "See?"

"Well, it's my house!" Zoe said. "So we have to play what I want!"

"That's not fair!" Elmo replied. "We can't always play what you want! Elmo wants to play in the sandbox!"

"Then maybe you should go by yourself!" said Zoe. "Because I don't *want* to play in the sandbox!"

"Fine! Elmo will just go!" Elmo said sadly. He took his sand toys and went to the playground.

Zoe sat at her table. She pretended to drink tea. She picked up a cookie and put it down again.

"A tea party is only fun with a friend," Zoe said unhappily. She gathered up her cups, saucers, and cookies. She put them into a basket and went to the playground.

Meanwhile, Elmo had been trying to build a sand castle. "Elmo needs Zoe's help to make it tall enough," he said sadly.

When Zoe arrived at the playground, she saw Elmo. "Are you still mad at me?" she asked.

"Elmo is mad *and* sad," Elmo replied. "Zoe was not very nice to Elmo. Zoe hurt Elmo's feelings."

"I'm sorry, Elmo," said Zoe. "Are you going to be mad forever? Or can we still be friends?"

"Elmo needs to be mad a little bit longer," he answered. "So Zoe should count to ten and then Elmo will not be mad anymore."

As Zoe counted, Elmo realized he was not mad or sad anymore. He was just glad to see Zoe.

"Ten!" Zoe called loudly. "Now what?"

"Now Elmo will hug Zoe," Elmo said as he hugged his friend. "Elmo is glad that Elmo and Zoe made up—but Elmo still wants to play in the sandbox and Zoe still wants to have a tea party."

"Let's have a tea party *in* the sandbox," Zoe suggested.

So Zoe climbed into the sandbox with her basket.
First she helped Elmo build a very tall sand castle. After that, Elmo helped her set up the tea party. Then the two friends drank pretend tea and ate some real cookies, which were delicious—sand and all!

Thank you, Elmo and Zoe, for that very friendly story! I will see you at the end of the book, okay? Perhaps we can get together later, after the book. . . .

Oh, hello again! You may have noticed that I, Grover, am now wearing a snowsuit. You may ask why I am wearing this warm, yet stylish, ensemble. That is a very good question. Turn the page and you will find out!

Hello, everybodee, from snowy Alaska! I, Grover, have traveled far away from Sesame Street on this dogsled, led by this cute and adorable doggie.
It is very cold in Alaska in the winter! Do you know the word for "winter" in Alaska? You do not? Well, then, I, Grover, will tell you! In Alaska, winter is called *ukiuq*.

It is now time for the Spanish Word of the Day with my friend Rosita. I wonder what word we will learn today. Oh, I am so curious!

¡*H*ola, *amigo!* That means "Hello, friend!" And *hola, amigos*. Hello, friends. Now you know that the Spanish Word of the Day is *amigo*. It means "friend."

Can you all say it with me? AH-MEE-GO. Good job!

Elmo is my *amigo*.

And Elmo is **your** *amigo,* too!

Zoe is a girl, so she is my *amiga*.

And you're my *amiga*, Rosita!

And together we are all *amigos*!

¡Adios, amigos!

Greetings! I am the Count. And I have written a little song all about the number four—because **4** is the Number of the Day!

One, two, three, four—
I just adore the number four.
All around are groups galore
Of things to count from one to four.
Bats, bananas, and more to see,
All in groups of four—not three!

Come on, let's count some more!

One, two, three, four—
Count four spiders on the floor!
The number four is really great.
Count four bananas on a plate!
Count to four, over and over,
Count four windows—
But just one Grover!

1 2 3 4

See that door on the next page? That door will lead us into Elmo's World. You know Elmo, right? He is cute and adorable, like yours truly, but he is red instead of blue. Let us knock and see if Elmo is home! Oh, I am so excited!

Welcome to Elmo's World! Elmo is so happy to see you!

Today Elmo is thinking about friends. Did you know that sometimes friends are a lot alike, and sometimes they are different? And either way is okay with friends!

Elmo's friends are very special because they make Elmo feel happy. Elmo drew these pictures.

This is Zoe.
Zoe is Elmo's best friend.
Zoe loves ballet.

Baby Bear and Telly are best friends.

So are Bert and Ernie.

And you are Elmo's friend, too!

And now there are no more pages left to turn. . . .

I hope that you have enjoyed this visit to *Sesame Street*. I, Grover, have enjoyed being your tour guide. You did an excellent job turning pages! Your cute and adorable little fingers must be very tired!

I cannot wait to see you again! Next time we will go somewhere warm and sunny, like Hawaii. If you thought I looked adorable in my snowsuit, wait until you see me in my grass skirt!

Good-bye for now, everybodee!